DARWISH
&
HAWAZIN

DARWISH

&

HAWAZIN

DR. MAHMOUD F. AL-ALI

ARPress
ILLUMINATING IDEAS
EMPOWERING VOICES

ARPress
45 Dan Road Suite 5
Canton MA 02021

Hotline: 1(800) 220-7660
Fax: 1(855) 752-6001

Ordering Information:
Quantity sales. Special discounts are available on quantity purchases by corporations, associations, and others. For details, contact the publisher at the address above.

Printed in the United States of America.

ISBN-13:   Paperback   979-8-89389-383-0
            eBook   979-8-89389-384-7

Library of Congress Control Number: 2024916715

DEDICATION

I would like to dedicate this book: *Darwish and Hawazin* to my grandsons and granddaughters:

Grandsons		**Granddaughters**	
Ali	Sewed	Subhan	Sewed
Mohammed	Sewed	Fatima	Sewed
Hassan	U.S.A.	Lyan	U.S.A.
		Sarah	U.S.A.
Hashim	U.K.	Fatima	U.K.
Fawzi	U.K.		
Hamza	JORDON		
Haider	JORDON		
Sadik	JORDON		

Hoping that they are studying hard and learning a lot in order to have a full education and to be in the future, each of them the second to none.

INTRODUCTION

This book is regarded as a masterpiece of the Society of Iraq. The theme and the content will appear through the four chapters of the story.

In *Chapter One:*

Darwish said "Of course, my father Haj Farman once told us that his father came to Baghdad with my mother, Al-Hajja Nafisa, and they lived in Bab al-seif area near Shawwaka, which is located in the Karkh area, He opened a shop selling spices, vegetables and certain agricultural crops needed by the people in the area of Al-Shawwaka at that time.

My father introduced me to (Mullah) during the Ottoman era. Mullah was a sort of school. In the first three months the child listened, then he moved to the memorizing. Last he moved to the stage of reading and writing. After graduating from the Mullah school. Darwish, worked with his father in the shop.

Years passed without much change. One day, Sheikh Bulaq came to the shop and met with my father Haj Farman.

I listened to his talk about what he and his tribe were suffering from the scarcity of water and wished to find a modern way to water the plants to increase the crop production. He said, "There is a wide piece of land that has not been developed yet. Because we lack a pump that transports water from the river to the land."

Later on, Darwish went to Sheikh Bulaq and made the agreement with him. Darwish should bring the water pump which remains as his property, and he gives them free of charge water for their land and plants, in return Sheikh Bulaq would provide Darwish with a group of peasants from among his tribe, to work with Darwish to cultivate other unused pieces of land.

At that time, Darwish was working with the peasants, around the clock without getting tired or bored. He directed them and supervised their work.

Hawazin, the Daughter of Sheikh Bulaq, occasionally brought Darwish food that included bread, onions, boiled eggs and some food for the villagers, which made him think of her more. Then the marriage will be taking place later. These were the traditions of the villagers to honor the guest.

Darwish and Hawazin had four sons and four daughters and then we will see their activities.

In *Chapter Two*:

A period of time passed and many, many events had occurred. It happened that the husband of Shamander, the oldest girl, invited the husbands of the other sisters, to spend an evening in the famous club in the city known as the Alwiya club for dinner in the club restaurant.

In *Chapter Three*:

In the Teachers institute, Zaidoon was one of the lecturers of English Language for one year. One day kawthar wanted to cheat in an examination but Zaidoon caught her and took the examination paper from her and asked her to leave the examination hall.

In *Chapter Four*:

The invasion occurred. The Iraqi army and police forces were abolished creating a tragic catastrophe. Iraqi borders were left unprotected. The extremists rushed into Iraq from all over the world. Iraq became a hotbed for all kind of gangs. Life in Iraq became unbearable.

Finally, the reader will find an interesting and unexpected ending.

The Author

CHAPTER ONE

While the family members were busy running their daily life, they heard happy voices and trills, followed by sudden knocking on the kitchen door. When the door was opened, Ashmim entered carrying a pot full of yogurt and her daughter Basima behind her carrying another pot of milk and butter. Both were happy because they had good news, namely the birth of one of the cows. Ashmim began to speak, "The cow gave birth to [A calf {newborn cow}], and I am here to give you the good news. Sheikh Darwish and Sheikha Hawazen would be very happy if they hear the good news."

Zafaran answered, "God willing, when they call us, we will give them the good news, and congratulations to you!"

Kawthar shouted, "Congratulations to you, come put the milk pots down so that we would boil the milk."

They put the pots on the kitchen table, and then the other girl, Sundus, came in and said: "Come, Nasima, take some plates of sweets."

After a while they left. It was one of the cold February days where the Sheikh Darwish family sat down chatting and listening to the music. The girls were busy preparing the table, making sweets and bringing the necessary supplies of nuts and whatever was needed for the chatting session that people are accustomed to at that time in the hall of the house. The house is situated in a city, that was previously a village called Dabash 50 miles away from the capital city of Baghdad.

Sheikh Darwish's house is set in an area full of agricultural lands and orchards. A spacious house with its multiple rooms. It was in the center of the city, surrounded with a large back garden full of fruit trees. At the rear end of the garden there was a shed for two cows. Near the shed lived a man and his wife who took care of the cows and milked them to produce yogurt, butter and cheese for Darwish's family. The sky became clear. While the family was in this setting, their uncle, Masroor Ibn al-Sheikh Bulaq visited them. In the conversation the girl called Shamandar asked: "Uncle, you know father's history since he came to this area. We want you to talk about this topic today."

Uncle Masroor, "after I drink my cup of tea, I'll talk about the history of your father Sheik Darwish."

Second girl, "We need to know the history of the father and his father, our grandfather Haji Farman, may God have mercy on his soul."

Third Girl, "We always remember his good deeds."

All family members said together that they were proud of him.

Masroor rose from his place and sat near the fireplace.

He began by saying, "Before we enter into the conversation, I would like to tell you that this city was previously a village. It was called by the name of my grandfather, Sheikh Dabbash."

Kawthar said, "Uncle, we hope that you talk about our grandfather, the father of our father."

Sheikh Masroor started to talk, "I accompanied Zarkash one day at dawn before sunrise. He was the peasant who used to drive the wagon loaded with crops. At that time, I was seven years old. We travelled in the crop wagon, which used to carry all the harvest to sell it to the city shops. Zarkash was used to drive the wagon to the city center where there were shops selling other supplies needed by the people of the city while we were on the road selling spices, vegetable, serials and other supplies needed by the city dwellers."

He continued, "While we were on the road, I asked Zarkash if he knew the people to whom we were going with the crop? He replied, 'Dear Masroor, I know the owner of the shop that we deal with, I know him well. He is called Haji Farman. He has a large shop, and he has three daughters and three sons. the oldest is called Darwish, then Hamdan and the youngest is Hardan. But Darwish was the most active among them. He was his father's right arm. His father relied on him in the running of the shop. I heard from close folks that their father bought a fishing boat. Some days Darwish used to go fishing, while Hamdan and Hardan worked in the shop. On our arrival we found the three brothers in the shop and I had the opportunity to get to know them, but I was leaned to get to know Darwish more. Truly, I found myself attracted to him because he was a young man with clear vitality characters and wide knowledge. Darwish invited me to accompany him in the fishing boat because we used to stay in the city center for a couple of days. We would go shopping for everything we need in the village and we would also get some rest from the trouble of the road. Next morning I went with Darwish on a fishing trip and I found him really an energetic young man. When we returned home, I relayed what happened to my father, your maternal grandfather, Sheikh Bulaq, may God have mercy on his soul, who was a friend of Haji Farman long ago. When I married your aunt Salousa, as I remember, we sent the invitation to Haji Farman, but he apologized. He sent his son Darwish to attend the wedding party. When he arrived on his stallion, we hosted him for ten days. This was the first visit and during this period he wandered around our agricultural areas. He became interested in our irrigation process. At the time the process relied on rain and some other very difficult primitive methods. Most of the conversations revolved around the scarcity of irrigation water. During the wedding Darwish stared at a beautiful little girl, who was singing and dancing distinctively with other children."

Uncle Masroor continued, "He was eager to talk to her, and she in turn gave him a good look, but he did not have the opportunity to talk to her. Darwish admired her for a long time. He heard some women calling her Hawazen. After the wedding ceremony, Darwish returned to his family. His second visit was a few years later, followed by other visits."

During uncle Masroor's chat, Darwish's second son, Fehmawi, knocked on the door. I opened the door for him, and he entered and gave his uncle Mansoor a warm greeting. As he had not seen him for a long time.

After he had tea, his uncle Masrour surprised him with the following question, "How are you doing? Some time ago we heard that you traveled to Cairo."

Fehmawi answered, "First I went to Beirut and enrolled in Al-Maqasid Secondary School. You know I was not lucky enough to pass the baccalaureate exams here. After a year of study, I traveled to Cairo and registered in the Faculty of Arts at Al-Azhar University. After a year I was transferred to Baghdad University, College of Arts. After graduation I was appointed as a civil servant. In short, I am not comfortable with the job."

Fehmawi continued, "In fact, I came to tell you that I received a telegram from my brother Wannas from London saying that father and mother completed their checks. Thank God they are in good health and will return after a week."

Shamandar, "Thank you, dear brother. We should be prepared to receive them."

Kawthar, "Sundus and Zafaran will arrange the hall and the living room, and we must inform Ashmim to reach her husband, Zirnikh, in order to arrange the garden and water the trees."

Zafaran, "I am happy. We will be happier when they come with gifts."

Sundus, "I think the gifts will be of a luxurious quality, and in general, Wannas is the one who is responsible for purchasing the gifts."

Masroor, "How is Wannas doing in UK?"

Fehmawi, "Wannas traveled to London before I traveled to Beirut. He enrolled in a college in London, but he needed to learn English at the time. He lived with a family consisting of a divorced woman with a child living with her parents. After nearly a year, my brother Wannas married the divorced woman, but this marriage was concealed from my father and mother. Wannas loved the football game, so he was busy studying and failed the exams. He dropped out of school. For many years he was dependent on financial assistance from my father. Father sent him a monthly amount sufficient for his living, until father and mother traveled to England for medical tests, when they found out."

There was knocking on the door. Masroor's son, Hazbar, came in asking for his father.

They were visited by guests who asked for Masroor. He got up, asked for permission to leave telling Zafaran that he would complete the story. He promised them that on the first opportunity he would continue the conversation and he left. While they were busy eating candies and nuts, they heard gunfire. Shamandar went to the kitchen. Suddenly, Zirnikh came and knocked on the kitchen door. Shamandar opened the door for him. He told her that he inquired about the gunfire. He was told those shots were from a party of joy held in one of the houses. He came to reassure them. She thanked him and he returned to his home located at the back garden. Shamandar assured the family. Later, Fehmawi spoke to the family about Zirnikh, a remarkable peasant, who did his job skillfully, saying, "You know this peasant Zirnikh is among the most faithful persons to our father. One day father told me about his story."

Kawthar asked, "what is Zirnikh's story?"

He answered her, "My understanding is Zirnich was one of the peasants who worked with father for a long time."

He continued, "One day while Zirnich was attending a farmer's wedding, one of the girls caught his attention. Her name was Ashmim, who was also attending the wedding and he liked her. After the wedding, he learned that the feeling was mutual. After a while he decided to go to her father Manati, the peasant, to propose to his daughter. Father denied his proposal a week later. When he asked for the reasons, he was told that Her uncle Sagar wanted her to marry one of his boys, knowing that she refuses categorically to marry his boy. She preferred to marry Zirnikh with whom she exchanged the same feeling. In the village things were moving against her wishes. It was a tradition called [prohibition]. According to this tradition a close relative can force his female cousin to marry him and prevent her from marrying any other person. Zirnich was in agony. He met her secretly and agreed with her that she should go to the mother Sheikha Hawazen to tell her to speak to Sheikh Darwish, my father, to find a solution for them. Soon she told the father who sent for Zirnikh and sought his opinion. He found him eager to marry Ashmim. The tradition of forbidding placed by her uncle Sagar was a roadblock. Father promised that he will do what he can to help Zirnich get married. Meanwhile father summoned the girl's father Manati and her uncle Sagar. He spoke to them and convinced them that this tradition is harming the family and causing problems. A family built on this tradition would be miserable. He advised them to approve the marriage of Ashmim to Zirnich. After a lot of effort, the two agreed. Afterwards he informed Zirnich of the good news and gave him a sum of money to prepare himself for marriage. Their marriage was accomplished. When mother and father wanted to buy the cows, he brought Zirnikh and Ashamim and settled them at the back garden to take care of the cows and the garden at the same time. They were loyal and honest on top of their dedication to their work. This is the story of Zirnikh and Ashamim. Of course, whenever a dilemma happened in the village, father used to study the problem and direct the village elders. In this case, father sent an invitation to the village dignitaries. When they came to his house, he began to talk to them about the necessity of abandoning this tradition of [prohibition] that prevents a girl to get married and that none of her relatives should have the right to forbid her marriage. Every girl has the right to agree or refuse. Then he moved his conversation to the need to respect women because they represent half of our society. Happiness of every family begins with a woman's happiness because when she is happy, the whole family is happy. Then, family problems are minimized, and vice versa. After spending the evening discussing this matter they left. As usual father kept talking about avoiding the prohibition, frequently, to benefit the villagers."

After this conversation Fehmawi got up to return to his family, saying, "I got to go home!"

He left the house and went with his younger brother Habbash toward the external door.

Three days later, their older brother Hamzawi visited them and inquired about the arrival of father and mother. He sat down to spend some time with them and talked to them about what happened to the children of a peasant when the first school was opened in the village. A peasant came complaining that his son Jallab was refusing to go to school. He brought him to our father to talk to him. At that time father was with a number of dignitaries. He asked the student Jallab about the reason. Jallab answered that he did not like going to school. His father interrupted him, saying that he liked only to play with the children. My father told him my son your future, not to mention your life, lies in going to school. Because with learning you will find happiness in life. Everything around us, we recognize only by learning. He directed his words to the audiance, saying, (*Remember the words of Imam Ali who said raise your children because they were created for a generation other than yours.*) Adults should encourage their children go to school because we want the next generation to be all educated. because with learning, they can taste the flavor of life and improve their living. Then Father gave Jallab an amount of money.

He promised him that if he went to school and learn, he would be provided with a job to earn a monthly salary. Jallab's heart was filled with joy and he promised not to drop out of school. Praise to God, after a while going to school became a normal habit. Even the children loved it.

After Hamzawi finished the story, his brother Habbash mentioned another tale, namely the tale of the schoolboy Ginfas, who used to drink alcohol and getting drunk. He disturbed his neighbors. When a neighbor came complaining. Father immediately summoned Ginfas and his father. When they showed up, he talked to them about the damage caused by drinking alcohol. He told them that he heard a medical report from one of the radios about the health problems caused by drinking alcohol and its effect on the kidneys. It also causes damage to the liver, in addition to the inconvenience caused by the actions of many people who call on his father to guide Ginfas give up drinking and consume fruit juice instead, which is useful and can cause no damage. At this point whole tale ended.

About a month after the return of Sheikh Darwish and his wife Sheikha Hawazen, the family happened to meet one evening, and this time they asked their father to talk about the family's heritage, and he agreed and started talking, "Of course, my father Haj Farman once told us that his father came to Baghdad with my mother, Al-Hajja Nafisa, and they lived in the Bab al-Seif area near Shawwaka, which is located in the Karkh area, He opened a shop selling spices, vegetables and certain agricultural crops needed by the people in the area of Al-Shawwaka at that time.

The first child was my older sister Najiba, followed by my sister Habiba then me and my brothers Hamdan and Hardan, then my sister Hassiba came last. When I was six years old, my father introduced me to [Mullah] during the Ottoman era.

Mullah was a sort of school. In the first three months the child listened, then he moved to the memorizing. Last he moved to the stage of reading and writing. After graduating from the mullah school, I worked with my father in the shop.

After a couple of years my sisters got married one after the other, and I was the right-hand man to deal with the peasants who brought crops to my father. We were in good terms with them.

It is worthwhile to mention that I was enjoying the love of my father and my mother Haja Nafeesa. This love was noted in a remarkable way by my brothers.

After a while we bought a fishing boat and worked in fishing as another source of income, but I was not convinced of this situation because I wished that our life would be better.

During the fishing sessions I thought about our life and how we could improve it to the better. Those thoughts crossed my mind especially when I was walking on the Riverbank. But all that was wishful thinking.

Years passed without much change. One day Sheikh Bulaq came to the shop and met with my father Haj Farman.

I listened to his talk about what he and his tribe were suffering from the scarcity of water and wished to find a modern way to water the plants to increase the crop production. he said, "There is a wide piece of land that has not been developed yet. Because we lack a pump that transports water from the river to the land.

This information remained in my mind until we were liberated from the Ottoman rule. As soon as the Ottomans evacuated, the British arrived!

While I was in the shop a customer came in and told me that one of the merchants imported water pumps to sell. It was at the end of 1918 and immediately I took from him the address of the merchant. Next day I went to him and asked about the prices of the pumps and how to install and use them. I took an idea about the matter. Back at home I took a long time to think about my next step. After a while I had the idea of working in fishing so that I could collect the amount I needed to buy the pump. I told my father who encouraged me to implement the idea that I talked about now and then.

In about two months my father summoned me and my brothers Hamdan and Hardan and gave me an amount of money that was enough to buy a water pump and asked me to take it to the village of Sheikh Bulaq.

He mentioned to me to sign an agreement with him on the basis that we bring him the pump and he pledges to send the whole crop to our shop.

When I came out of the shop I decided to travel to the village and agreed with Sheikh Bulaq. To implement the agreement, I went back to the city and bought the pump and took it to the village. Next day I went immediately to Sheikh Bulaq. In his office we talked about agriculture and confirmed the agreement with him. I should bring the water pump which remains as our property. It was decided that we give them free of charge water for their land and plants, in return he would provide us with a group of peasants, from among his tribe, to work with me to cultivate other unused pieces of land.

He agreed whereupon I brought the seeds with me. This time I prepared to live in the village to supervise the work personally. Therefore, I set up a cottage for my residence.

I used to wake up at dawn along with the peasants. I started digging the necessary water streams and we started spreading the seeds in the proper seasons. We had the water flowing in the streams to be used whenever we needed at all the times. We completed our job and waited for the harvest day. The crops were unexpectedly abundant.

I forgot to mention that your mother, Sheikha Hawazin, occasionally brought me food that included bread, onions, boiled eggs and some food for the villagers, which made me think of her more. These were the traditions of the villagers to honor the guest.

At that time, I was working with the peasants, around the clock without getting tired or bored. I directed them and supervised their work.

The news of my father's illness came to me as a surprise! I prepared to return to the city and while I was on the way my father passed away. I attended his burial ceremony. Before I returning to my work in the village, I agreed with my brothers that they continue working in the shop and I decided to go back and work to expand planting and I bought other pumps and increased the number of the peasants and I planted other large pieces of land. We planted palm trees, citrus trees such as oranges, lemons, grapefruits and other fruit like pears, apricots and peaches.

One day I sat down in the cottage and pondered about work. I felt that I needed to marry Hawazin, the beautiful daughter of Sheikh Bulaq. Because I loved her. After a while I decided to come back and told my family about my intention. But I did not expect the negative reaction of my family. When my mother heard my intention, she refused first and wondered why I was not thinking of marrying one of the city girls. She advised me to abandon the idea of marrying the village girl. I told her that I want to marry the daughter of Sheikh

Bulaq, my late father's friend. She answered, "But, my son, this girl you want to marry follows the customs and traditions of the primitive village while the daughters of the city are civilized. They follow the customs and traditions of the city." I told her that this was not a problem because she can learn. After a few days I managed to convince her and my brothers also. but my sisters Najiba and Habiba were determined to refuse while Hassiba was hesitant at first, but when I convinced my mother she agreed as well.

I went back to my work and proceeded to Sheikh Bulaq to ask for his daughter Hawazin's hand. He asked and obtained her consent. I built a house for us and we celebrated our wedding. We were married and we lived and worked together to build our future. We started delivering water and planted other pieces of land. Hawazin was a good help to me. She used the mill to produce flour and baked bread. Sometimes she helped in digging irrigation streams and even in harvesting the crop.

When Sheikh Bulaq saw our efforts in cultivating the abandoned land, he decided to gather the elders of the village and discussed with them to grant Darwish the title of Sheikh. They agreed and held a ceremony attended by a group of villagers and Sheikh Bulaq announced his decision to grant the title of Sheikh to Darwish, as well as the title of Sheikha to Hawazin. Ever since the people in the village have been calling them as such, thus increasing the activity of Sheikh and Sheikha Hawazin.

Thereafter we expanded the cultivation of most of the land that was not cultivated before. When Sheikha Hawazin got pregnant, I was happy and dreamt of our first child. Unfortunately, she aborted, because she was working very hard. She decided to go back and live in the city. I traveled with my wife and stayed with my family for two months. We moved to a new house which I bought and took my mother to live with us. The first thing I did was bringing a "Mullaya" to teach Sheikha Hawazin how to read and write.

I also used the skills of my mother and sister hassiba to teach Sheikha Hawazin the city lifestyle. After a short period Hawazin became as if she was born in the city.

After a short while my brothers Hamdan and Hardan married and each of them lived in a house of his own.

In 1930 our first child, Hamzawi, was born. In 1935 our second child, Shamandar, was born. and in 1940 we welcomed our third child, Fehmawi. Zafaran, our fourth child, came in 1943. In1945 Wannas was born in 1949. Kawthar was born in 1950 followed by Sandus. I missed to mention that my relationship with my two sisters Najiba and Habiba has not been good since I married Hawazin and the dispute between us continued even though my mother and sister Hassiba were on my side, and I was following a system in my life to solve every problem I encounter following traditional methods. If I were unable to solve it, I would leave it for another opportunity to give myself more time to think. If I fail, time will take care of it. A few months later, we heard that one of my older sisters' son died drowning in the river.English translation.

We took this terrible opportunity to visit her and stood by her side to console her and minimize the pain of the calamity. The visit normalized relations between me and my sisters. I was keen on continuing the good relations. I was always going to the village to supervise the work of the peasants and guide them. A year came when the State surveyed the land and registered its ownership. I accompanied the special committee for land registration that took about three months to survey our land. The committee found that the property is measured at thousands of dunums and was registered in the name of our father Sheikh Darwish. But this time another problem popped up. The problem this time was with my brothers Hamdan and Hardan. Once they heard that the land was registered under my name, they demanded a share in the property that I developed alone. Initially they demanded a 50:50 share. I rejected. After a short period, intermingled with disagreements, threats and quarrels with my brothers, I agreed, because, I thought about the issue and realized that it was better to involve my brothers with me in order to manage this vast property.

A year passed after the Second World War and situation calmed down. The road to our village became better than before. Buses were run by government and a bus reached the village.

We decided to bring surveyors to plan and convert a large piece of our land into residential areas. The land was divided into 100 meters per piece for sale. After the streets and alleys were identified, we the three brothers decided to live there. I constructed a spacious house where we now live. My brothers built their large houses in the opposite area.

To encourage house building, we offered some people pieces of land free of charge, provided they built houses. Houses were constructed until the land became a residential area. Then we published advertisements for sale at affordable prices. There was a rush to purchase. We named this village (City of Sheikh Darwish). We learned that the news reached our sisters who became upset because they said that this success is all thanks to the father Haj Farman who paid you the money to purchase the first pump.

For appeasement purposes, we gave every sister a piece of land. Then harmony prevailed, which we were keen to maintain. We continued to achieve success in the sale of land and expanding the city.

Then there was a change in our country's regime from the royal system to a republic.

The new regime confiscated a lot of our land under the pretext that they wanted to build projects on the land. We had no right to object. We continued to sell from our land. A number of schools were opened in the city, in addition to a clinic, a police station and a football field.

The means of transportation have improved and helped a lot of people to move and live in the city. In recognition of the support provided to us by Hawazin, her father, brothers and many of their people, we decided to change the name of the city to the (City of Darwish and Hawazin.) Moreover, they made efforts over the past years.

The narrative of Sheikh Darwish continued until dawn!

CHAPTER TWO

A period of time passed and many, many events had occurred. It happened that the husband of Shamander, the oldest girl, invited the husbands of the other sisters, to spend an evening in the famous club in the city known as the Alwiya Club for dinner in the club restaurant.

While the men were at the club, it happened that the sisters gathered in the home of the oldest one to chat about their memories.

The oldest sister said, "I remember when Hammash and his family came to ask for my sister's hand, Kawthar, who was a high school student. That was at the beginning of 1969. After deliberation we informed them of our approval. Preparations were made for the engagement. Hammash was an officer in the police force.

Kawthar interrupted saying, "Hammash is born in 1943. We spend our honeymoon in northern Iraq. After a short period of time, Hammash enrolled in the evening law school to obtain a bachelor's degree in law. he was ambitious to have a better future."

Then Shamandar resumed the conversation, "My sister Sundus, who was also a high school student, became engaged also in 1970, when Zaidoon and his family asked for her hand. The engagement lasted about a year.

Sundus spoke, "Zaidoon was born in 1947. We spent our honeymoon in Istanbul. I still remember the first time he spoke to me he said that we must adapt to becoming a family with special and distinctive features different from the rest of the families, when we returned home, Zaidoon went to work. In the morning he was a clerk of the Government offices, in the evening he was a third-year student at the Faculty of Arts, English Literature Department. He was smart, full of energy and ambitious. He read a lot and longed for a better future."

Shamandar resumed, "But Zafaran, who had graduated from the Institute of Home Rehabilitation, was admired by my Husband's friend, Waddah, who was a young graduate of the Institute of Industrial Engineering and was working in an industrial factory near our city. that was in mid-1971."

Zafaran interrupted saying "Waddah, born in 1945, was very ambitious. After our marriage he attempted to go to evening college to get his bachelor's degree in engineering, but the factory needed him. He had to try another time."

When Sundus asked about the story of Shamandar's marriage story, who was a secondary school student, Shamandar answered, "In 1953 my cousin Salman (My aunt Habiba's son) visited us with his folk and asked for my hand and soon we were married. Salman was born in 1930. He was a primary school teacher, but he continued his studies in the evening. He graduated from the faculty of law and practiced law. Afterwards he opened a realty office in our city. From this work we earned more money. We built the house we are living in and we bought a motor vehicle. We have boys and girls at school, and we lead a happy family life."

The three women had gathered in their oldest sister's house because her husband Salman had invited their husbands Hammash, Zaidoon and Waddah to the city club called Alawia Club, a social cultural sports club founded in 1924 on the banks of the Tigris River on the Rasafa side of Baghdad. The club is considered one of the oldest institutions and clubs in Baghdad. It includes beautiful gardens and also a number of halls for club members to pass a good time. Salman's invitation was in late 1972. After each of them took a tour in the club facilities to watch some sports events they sat down around a table in one the club halls. Salman welcomed them and thanked them for accepting his invitation to spend time in the club and they began to chat.

Hammash asked the host, "How did you get to know Shamandar before marriage?

He replied, "Shamandar is my uncle's daughter (Darwish). one day I saw her while she was in front of one a store shopping. I saluted her and we had a chat and I liked her. a couple of days later I asked my mother to arrange my engagement to her. She welcomed the idea and so things were done easily in those days. We got married. Salman in his turn asked, "how did you meet Kawthar?"

Hammash replied, "One day I went to the high school to accompany my sister on our way home. My sister came out chatting with her colleague, Kawthar. I saluted them and my sister introduced me to her friend. I liked her and I admired her more when I learned that she was the daughter of Darwish. But when I asked my parents to arrange my engagement to her, they declined at the beginning. The reason was the difference in our social and economic status. Because father was a policeman with a limited income. Although I was a graduate of the Police Academy and I was a police officer with limited income, I insisted to have the engagement arranged. Thank God, everything worked and we got married."

"And you Zaidoon how were you introduced to Sundus before marriage."

Zaidoon answered, "While I was attending a wedding party, Sundus came with her mother and they saluted us and we sat at the same table, because my mother was a relative of theirs. I got the opportunity to talk to her. I admired her and we got engaged. I decided to get married after one year so that we can get to know each other more. After the engagement period we got married. It is your turn Waddah to talk about the same topic."

Waddah answered, "I visited my friend's house, Salman, and it happened that Zafaran was visiting her sister. That offered me the opportunity to chat with her. I admired her and my admiration got bigger when I knew she was the daughter of Sheikh Darwish. After the special ceremonies we got married."

The conversation went on in this context. We had ice cream and a soft drink and had a good time at the club. We decided to meet next week again.

After a week we arrived at the club and we were eager to have a good time watching the activities of the club. We wandered through the corridors of the club until it was time for dinner. After dinner, the four of us were seated, Salman talked about his uncle's situation, "Unfortunately, my uncle's children are the opposite of their father the Sheikh. Their father was smart and clever. My mother says compared to his relatives and his peers he was superior to them all. But his children were not like him whether in smartness or vitality. For example, Hamzawi did not graduate from primary school. When he failed the official exams (Baccalaureate), his father found him a job in a farm to supervise the peasant's work. He made no progress this until he married the daughter of his uncle Hamdan. His father gave him a piece of land and built him his house and then after a couple of years he opened a shop for him. But he made no success in the business. He remained the same without making any progress. Between now and then his father would give him a piece of land to sell and live on the sale revenue. His other son Fehmawi was unable to complete study in this country. He went to Beirut and then to Cairo. After his return, he barely completed his study in the Social department. Then he married one of the students. He was employed for a short period of time. He quarreled with an employee and he left the job. Their father opened a tourist company for him and his brother Hamzawi."

"Zaidoon and I visited in their company a while ago" said Hammash.

Zaidoon said, "We visited them and had coffee with them in their tourist office, but it seems to be the office was new. I think working in the company requires experience to compete with other tourism companies."

Salman said, "They say we have employees with experience in this field. They appointed a beautiful secretary and I heard that Hamzawi and Fehmawi were competing for her friendship. As for Habbash, the youngest of Sheikh Darwish's sons, he was in high school and made no success until he was helped by private teachers in most subjects. He graduated from high school at low rates that did not qualify him for college. Yet they have a sense of fake superiority. You will notice that when you contact them. Hadbash had to depend on his father to find him a job to work. He worked with his father in the land sales office. He often took power of attorney from his sisters to complete the transactions, because my uncle Darwish had registered many plots of land in the names of his daughters, to evade paying state taxes. Habbash's work was to help one of the sons of the peasants to cut these large areas into small pieces to be sold and the revenue would go to Sheikh Darwish and part of it to Habbash who became rich, even before his marriage to his cousin, which happened thereafter.

Speaking to us when we visited them on occasions, Sheikh Darwish declared that he was selling what could be sold in his life. After his death, the unsold properties shall remain in the names of his daughters.

He had registered pieces of land for each girl. It is noticeable that he granted Zafaran five pieces of land each a thousand square meters. But to Sundus, who was known as a goodhearted daughter, he granted a piece of land measured as 250 dunums. His other daughters received only regular pieces of land."

Hammash asked Habbash, "How are you doing in the realty business?"

He said, "At the beginning our work was going through a normal phase, but after a couple of years of making profits, we faced some difficulties, because uncle Darwish started to make things difficult for us. For example, when we sell 50 lots of land, we prepare paperwork for the buyers. My uncles Hamdan and Hardan sign the papers of sale easily, but uncle Darwish delays signing at first. After Shamandar makes some efforts, uncle Darwish signs a few days later."

Hammash said, "In your opinion, Salman, what's the reason for these difficulties?"

Salman replied, "After a period of this dealing, I discovered that my uncle and his children do not like the husbands of the girls to be richer than them. Specially those who were not lucky either in school or at work. It was envy and jealousy on the one hand and their feeling of inferiority on the other."

"But the wealth of Sheikh Darwish's children is not little" said Zaidon. Salman replied, "This is true, but if you want to research how they got this money, you will see that it is not with their efforts. Their father knows that they did make it at their work, he provided them from time to time with pieces of land, they sell to run their lives. When my uncle saw that I work hard and make profits and I was very much critical of them, he started to feel the resentment along with his children. He asked me to stop selling but I did not respond to his request. Whenever I had the opportunity to sell a number of pieces of land, and was able to complete the transactions by uncles Hamdan and Hardan, Shamandar and I would go to uncle Darwish's house and spend strenuous efforts to convince him to the sign the transaction. The job was completed and the piece of land was sold and so every few months we do the same work that has generated profits we never imagined before."

Zaidon, "This is surprising, especially when you are his nephew (His sister's son) and at the same time the husband of his eldest daughter."

Salman, "Because when I saw my uncle's lazy children who were making no progress at school or at work, I used to blaming them and urging them to make more efforts, and in general, over time, you'd recognize this situation when you came into contact with them."

Hammash, "When we meet with them, they hide this fact, but many times and through their conversations we smell it. Anyway, over the years, it would probably become clearer."

Salman, "I'm sure you'll notice their empty greatness."

Zaidon, "In the future we will get to know them better."

Waddah, "I think it is getting late. God willing, we will meet at another opportunity. Thank you, Salman, for this invitation. Through what you said, we can conclude that self-employment is better than a limited salary job."

Salman, "Of course, self-employment is better, especially if the person has academic qualifications that may generate a lot of profits as well. We hope to meet all the time and repeat coming to the club."

Everyone agreed and the gathering came to an end.

At a time when Salman was busy in his office, Wadah, Zaidon and Hammash met in the house of Sheikh Darwish and left their wives in the house with Sheikha Darwish. They went to the Alawia Club. They sat down to have tea and chat, Zaidoon asked Hammash, "I see you are fluctuating. Do you believe in the unknown?" He answered, "I am only concerned with money-making. What I care about is making money by any means whatsoever. I have read a lot about the unknown and I have not made up my mind to give my opinion. Maybe that will materialize in my mind in the future."

Zaidoon directed the same question to Waddah who replied that he believes in scientific theory and frankly he admires Marxism that does not believe in the unknown. Then Hammash said, "and you Zaidon do you believe in the unknown?" He answered without hesitation, "I have read a lot about this subject, which is no longer ambiguous because it is confirmed with evidence and facts."

Hammash, "Can clarify more?"

Zaidon answered, "Of course, if by the unknown we mean the unseen things that are not seen by the naked eye and are not visible this is what science believes in. But there are things that cannot be seen with naked eye and science believe in also and they exist and we feel the.."

Waddah interrupted saying, "The topic needs to be clarified. What are these things?"

Zaidon replied, "like the air. We all sense it and we cannot live without, but we do not see it. Another example, is the human mind which humanity cannot live without."

The two paid attention to this conversation and Zaidon continued saying, "Not all that is unseen is not recognized. For example, if we look at the systems contained in our bodies, each operating with utmost accuracy, we must realize that this did not come from a vacuum. It is created and made to work with such precision by something. On the other hand. If we look at the earth, which is suspended in the air, orbiting around itself at a speed of 26 KM per minute and orbiting around the sun at a speed of 30 KM per second, we have wonder who suspended it and how it got suspended. Especially it makes three movements at the same time revolving around itself and orbiting around the sun and then moving with the sun horizontally to an unknown destination. Then this argument convinces me of the existence of a creator. This is confirmed by all the prophets who were sent to the people throughout the ages. Then is it possible that the three determined prophets: Moses, Jesus and Muhammed, came from a vacuum? Note that the period between one and the other is more than 500 years and each of them has brought a holy book that played a role in guiding the people and each of them still has followers. The common denominator between these three prophets is that they came with one clear message to all humanity because all human beings are one nation..."

Waddah interrupted asking, "Do you believe in the obsolete religious rituals they practice?"

Zaidon replied, "No because most of the religious rituals were the result of the religious heritage practiced by preachers, sultans, sorcerers, fake prophets, and priests throughout ages, but religion remains pure and free of impurities..."

Waddah interrupted, "What do you think is their message to the human beings?"

Zaidon replied: "It boils down to a few things: first faith in God, the creator of everything and capable of everything; the second is good deed. Everything that exists in this universe is created, especially since the theory of the cell has been refuted and has no scientific grounds. If you follow Scientific proofs you will reach the truth that the creator of this universe is God."

After this interesting conversation, the three of them left the club and went back to Sheikh Darwish's house each to take his wife home. Everyone talked to his wife about what happened between them. Soon Sheikh Darwish knew about the conversation. He liked Zaidoon and spoke to his wife Sheikha Hawazin.

Hammash flattered Sheikh Darwish and Sheikha Hawazin, but they considered Zaidon as a balanced person. Two years later, Hammash bought a house in Rasafa area near Sheikh Darwish city, while Zaidoon bought a house in Mansour, Al-Karkh. Sheikh Darwish provided assistance to Hammash and Zaidoon.

But Waddah lived in the same city in one of Sheikh Darwish's houses. This angered his sons who were unwilling to share their father's wealth with anybody. Criticism began and quickly turned into hatred which started nibling at their hearts. Then hatred turned toward the husbands of their sisters. It manifested itself in their remarks and actions.

For example, Fehmawi showed his resentment when his father helped Hammash to purchase a car. He also showed his resentment when his mother gave his sister Zafaran a few items from her father's house.

This is how the relations went between brothers and sisters, although compliments were prevailed sometimes, especially when a strange thing happened. Two of Hamzawi's children got sick and the family was sad. Especially when Fehmawi's daughter and son were inflicted with the same disease. The family focused on this disease for which the doctor found no cure when they took the sick children to London hospitals.

But when the disease started to get worse gradually until they died, the Shiek Darwish remembered what his father Haj Farman had said about a disease among his family for which there was no cure. But the disease inflicts his male grandchildren. Things worsened, when his son Habbash married his cousin and the disease inflicted his firstborn who died a few years later. But they all succumbed to the status quo and later they had boys and girls. They were relieved of the calamity that hit them. This is how the family lived.

CHAPTER THREE

In 1974, Zaidoon graduated from the college with excellent grades. He was appointed a lecturer of the English language in other departments of the college.

During the same year, a female teacher's institute was established coincidently. Two high school graduates, Sundus and Kawthar, were enrolled in the institute as students. Two years later they graduated and were employed as teachers in the primary school of the town.

In the Teachers Institute, Zaidoon was one of the lecturers of English laguage for one year. One day Kawthar wanted to cheat in an examination. But Zaidoon caught her and took the examination paper from her and asked her to leave the examination hall.

Kawthar went to visit her parents and complained and cried because of this incident. Her father Sheikh Darwish commended Zaidoon for his action and scolded her. Her husband Hammash swayed. He sympathized with his wife, but he knew that Zaidoon did the right thing. At the same time, he was careful not to anger her.

Waddah was admitted to the course opened in the University College during that year. Zaidoon was a teacher of English Language and he was one of the lecturers. After a year Zaidoon was admitted to one of the British universities to complete his higher education. He travelled to London to join the University at the beginning of 1976. After hard work he was awarded a master's degree in English literature. He was a hard worker and smart. His supervisor advised him to continue his studies to get his Doctorate Degree in the comparative literatures. During his study he met with many people of multiple cultures and different religions. He had the opportunity to read various books including the Old and New Testaments and some archaeological books, until he grasped the concept that reality lies in both worldly and eternity lives. Because God's prophets Moses, Jesus and Mohammed all informed us that there is an eternal life after death. The same goes to previous prophets. We must prepare for both lives. The prophets came to guide people to worship God and make good deeds. That is the thing that build man the right way and build the family and society in the earthly life and it is the right way to win both the earthly eternal lives. This is found in the Holy Book:

> (Did I not enjoin on you, O Ye children of Adam, that ye
> should not worship Satan, for that he was to you an enemy
> a vowed? And that ye should worship Me, {for that} this way
> the right way).

This increased his faith in the creator and good work that led to win both the eternal lives.

Zaidoon noticed that even the majority of civilized communities respect the laws, a faction of these people dodge the laws to evade paying taxes and resort to cheat others to make profits, also using drugs which are a reason for a lot of crimes occurring in the society.

Therefore, Zaidoon thought that when law and belief in God prevail according to the teachings of the prophets and messengers, at that time every person will become his own overseer. Full belief that God hears and sees is one of requirement for faith in God. On this basis the society becomes more civilized and get closer to perfection.

Zaidoon returned home in 1980. In this year Iraq-Iran war broke out. It continued for eight years.

Zaidoon was appointed as a professor in the university to teach English Language and Literature. He gained his student's admiration and his fellow professors' respect because he was well mannered and, at the same time, he was recognized for his wide knowledge.

When the time for the Iraqi Educational Society elections came, some of his fellow professors nominated him for the presidency of the Society. As a matter of fact, he was elected with highest votes.

He designed a working plan to implement the educational program he had prepared. Educational symposiums and conferences were held which increased the cultural activity in the country. This increased the admiration of the high rank at the Ministry of Education towards him.

On the other hand, even Sheikh Darwish was among his admirers. His sons Hamzawi, Fehmawi and Habbash and even Hammash noticed that admiration with resentment and jealousy. Extreme hatred toward Dr. Zaidoon ate their hearts out. But they hid their hatred and pretended to treat him nicely.

Hammash had completed his legal studies the year before, also Waddah completed his course. This was a proof to the family that its daughters' husbands were able to make progress by obtaining their degrees, while the sons missed the boat and were not so lucky with their education.

One day Sheikh Darwish summoned his sons and spoke to them as following, "I have heard that you get into your black moods when I help your sisters or their husbands."

Fehmawi, "Father's responsibility is to offer whatever he has to his sons, not to others..."

Sheikh Darwish interrupted him, "Well! If everyone of you asked himself what good he has done to his sons. Did you work hard continuously to succeed and build yourselves without help? What would your answer be? Of course, the answer is absolutely negative!"

"I'll start with Hamzawi. First, he failed at school. After we brought him to work in the farm, he did not stay there for a long time. He asked us to open for him a business shop. After a short time, he left the shop and decided to work with his brother in a tourist company. Instead of taking care of the company and develop the business he started to compete with his brother to gain the friendship of the secretary. This is Hamzawi's career."

"Fehmawi, after making a lot of efforts he graduated from college and was employed. Instead of adapting to the job, he disputed with his fellow employees and left his job. He worked with Hamzawi at the tourist company. Instead of focusing on the tourist business and work with his brother to increase the company's activities he started to compete with his brother to gain the friendship of the secretary."

"What about Wannas? what did he achieve in the past years and what educational degrees did he get? He went hanging around and playing as if he had gone to have fun and got married and built a family. He lived with his family on the money I used to send him every month."

"In spite of all the money we spent on Habbash's private tuition, he was unable to get a grade that would have qualified him for admission to any college. I brought him with me to work in the realty office.

This is the reality. You all depend on your father and his property. None of you is using his mind as he should."

Consider the husbands of your sisters! look at Salman's efforts! He prospered educationally and made his best efforts in his career for the sake of his family. Now he owns money with the sweat of his forehead.

Hammash also thrived educationally and prospered in his career as a policer officer.

Waddah graduated from the Engineering Institute. He was not satisfied with the educational gaps. He earned his college degree and became an engineer working in a government factory.

Dr. Zaidoon was a civil servant and a student when he got married. He studied hard at the college until he graduated with high grades. He was employed in the same college and he continued teaching and utilized his best efforts to get admission from a British university. Then he travelled and did his best at the university and received his PhD. Now, he is a university professor.

Haven't you noticed the difference between you and them? Do not blame me if I helped any of them? You'd better blame yourselves!

Then the Sheikh took the opportunity of the presence of his daughters in the house to speak to them, "I want to inform you of my opinion about you" he said.

He paused, "In my opinion, Sundus is the best, and I wish you all follow her example. I am speaking about her character which you all know very well."

In the beginning of Summer 1981 Salman purchased a new car and took his family into vacation to Turkey for one month by car. But a tragic calamity happened during their return. He was driving his car with fast speed. He crashed into a truck and passed away. His family survived and returned home. Ceremonies of mourning and grief were held for the loss suffered by the family.

In 1985 Sheik Darwish got sick. He was examined by many physicians and many medications were prescribed for him. He remained sick for a few days until he passed away.

Hammash took this opportunity to befriend the sons of Sheikh Darwish. He visited Habbash's office frequently with the hope of getting any financial resource but to no avail.

Hammash's income remained limited against the endless demands of his wife Kawthar. Because she was looking at her sisters, and the wives of her brothers, enjoying their expensive jewels, wearing expensive clothes and each of them driving their own cars. They are living extravagantly while she lives a humble life of a normal teacher with limited income.

Her sister, Sundus, was also a teacher, but she was in better situation than Kawthar, because Dr. Zaidon was paid a university professor's salary and he established an office in Mansour offering translation, printing, and photocopying services. Because it was the only office at that time, he got many clients. This was an additional source of income.

That is why Kawthar scolded her husband and hustled him to get her all the requirements of high life. Because Hammash income was limited, he was forced to take bribes to cover his wife's expenses.

After three months, the police department found out about his corruption. He was sacked from the police force. He had no choice but to start a law office. After a couple of years, he could not do more than feed his family.

He remained in good terms with a group of police officers. He worked as a lawyer and took advantage of his eloquence, he befriended Habbash who ran a realty business.

Habbash had friends within factory owners and Hammash became acquainted with them. He accompanied him and was introduce to owners of the factories. He knew from them that, because of scarcity of some raw materials, during the war period, they purchased them from the black market.

He became a snitch and passed this information to his friends, the police officers. The factory owners were arrested. He approached their families and promised them to get them out of jail for a sum of money.

With this conspiracy he made some money to provide a good life for his family for years.

Waddah continued to work as an engineer in the same lab and from time to time he would visit Dr. Zaidoon in his office and convey to him the family news. Because he was busy, sometimes teaching, and other times working in his office. This produced envy and jealousy in the heart of not only Sheikh Darwish's children, but even in the heart of Hammash who was increasing his flattery to Dr. Zaidoon and criticizing the works of both Habbash and Fehmawi.

Confidentially, he conspired with the children of Sheikh Darwish in any way that could harm Dr. Zaidoon.

In 1988 the war ended, and some tourist companies decided to reactivate the tourist movement, among those tourist companies was the tourist company of Hamzawi and Fehmawi.

A celebration was held by those tourist companies, guests included many people, interested in tourism in the country. Among the invitees were Waddah and Hammash. Dr. Zaidoon apologized because of his preoccupation in the university and society in addition to his office work.

During the ceremony Waddah explained to some of the guests that he had a hobby in the tourist attractions, and then he talked with Fehmawi and Hamzawi saying, "If you want to encourage travel and tourism, you must promote the business, especially that Iraq has the advantage of containing the ruins of some ancient civilizations such as:

The Ishtar Gate was the eighth gate to the inner city of Babylon. It was constructed in about 575 BCE by order of King Nebuchadnezzar II on the north side of the city. It was part of grand walled processional road leading into the city.

And the Tower of Babel narrative in Genesis II: 1-9 is an original myth meant to explain why the world's peoples speak different languages. According to the story, a united human race in the generations following the Great Flood, speaking a single language, and migrating eastward, comes to the land of Shinar.

Speaking state and cultural area based in central southern Mesopotamia. A small Amorite ruled state emerged in 1894 BCE, which contained the minor administrative town of Babylon.

Mesopotamia is a region of southwest Asia in the Tigris and Euphrates river system that benefitted from area's climate and geography to host the beginnings of human civilization.

The Akkadian Empire was the first ancient empire of Mesopotamia, after the long-lived civilization of Sumer. It was centered in the city of Akkad and its surrounding region. The Akkadian and Sumerian united empire speakers under one rule.

One of the most important economic divisions of Iraq is its ancient mosques and religious shrines. For example, Najaf is the most important city where religious tourism thrives.

Imam Ali Shrine

The Sanctuary of Imam Ali also known as the Mosque of Ali located in Najaf, Iraq, is a Muslim mosque housing the tomb of "Ali ibn Abi Talib," the cousin of Prophet Muhammad and the first Imam after him.

Millions of people used to visit Imam Ali on every occasion in every year.

Also, **the City of Karbala.**

The Holy Shrine of Imam Hussain

The Imam Hussain Shrine or the Place of Imam Hussian ibn Ali is the mosque and burial site of Hussain ibn Ali, He is the third Imam of Moslems.

Twenty million visitors used to visit Imam Hussain every occasion of his forty day in every year.

Waddah continued, "If you do tourism advertising and focus on these features and other tourism features in the country, the company shall witness a boom and you will make a lot of profits.

After the party everybody returned to his home.

After about two years Habbash invited the family, excluding Sundus and her husband. They deliberated the question of 250 donums of land which remained under Sundus' name.

Habbash said, "This land, which is under Sundus' name, is worth millions, meaning that she and her husband will be richer than all of us. I gathered you her today to think of a way to grab this piece of land and divide it between the family members in a legal way.

Fehmawi answered, "I agree with you."

Hamzawi said, "But this is her legal and legitimate right."

Habbash, "We could change that if we planned it well. Instead of her owning the land alone, it will be our own."

Zafaran said, "We ladies agree with Habbash. The land should be divided between the family members.

Hamzawi spoke, "If we could convince Sundus, Dr. Zaidoon will refuse relying on the fact that the land is an inheritance from her father. Of course, Sundus will support her husband. It looks like this matter is difficult to achieve..."

Hammash interrupted, "There's no problem an attorney cannot solve!"

Habbash said, "Tell us, Mr. attorney, how to solve this problem?"

Hammash said, "The solution consists of two parts. First, the ladies will inform Sundus that Sheikh Darwish had told them, before his death, that it was his will that the land should be divided between the family members not just for Sundus to keep."

He continued, "The second part of the solution, Habbash will convince her to sign a cheque for five millions, at which point Dr. Zaidoon will be in front of the *fait accompli*, and of course a check with such a big amount must be signed before the judge in order for the check to be effective."

Habbash, "This is a good idea, and we have to implement it. Each of us will play his role. We should wait for the right opportunity to do it."

Hammash, "Dr. Zaidoon informed me that next week he will travel to London to attend a conference. I guess the conference is scheduled for one week.

Habbash. "This will be the right opportunity."

Zafaran, "I'll call Sundus on the first day her husband travels, if God wills." Kawthar, "I'll also talk to her."

Habbash, "After she gets an idea about the mater, I'll pay her a visit in the morning. Then I'll accompany her to court, and I'm going to convince her to sign the check before the judge."

Hamzawy, "This way we will sell the land and distribute the revenue to everyone."

Habbashk pretending, "Of course, you know that Dr. Zaidoon's income is high and he has a prestigious career, a university professor, and his office makes a high income. If we give the land to Sundus in this case, she and her husband will be richer."

This scheme was executed during her husband's absence. After Dr. Zaidoon's return, he knew about this conspiracy and learned that it was designed by Habbash. Two days after his arrival Hammash visited him in his translation office and informed him. As usual he pretended to be on his side. Dr. Zaidoon thought that Hammash's intention was to drive a wedge in their relationship.

Dr. Zaidoon inquired from his wife Sundus and learned the truth, he told her that she had to use her mind and not to rush passionately in this mess.

He decided to understand from Habbash, what made him to behave that way against his father's will.

When he met with Habbash, he said to him, "Why did you do this?

Habbash, "I visited my sister and took her with me to secure our money."

Dr. Zaidoon, "In this shameful way, fraud, conspiracy and deception you made her to sign a cheque for 5 Million Dinars!"

Habbash, "My sister agreed to sign the check, so what is wrong with that?" Dr. Zaidoon, "But you forced her with conspiracy and lies. The method you used with Sundus, is despicable and disgraceful."

Habbash, "But this is a way to ensure that our money returns to us."

Dr. Zaidoon, "This is the right of Sundus as Sheikh Darwish's will. "But you want to usurp it greedily and ravenously."

Habbash, "But before his death, he said all these plots of land are for the family, not for individuals."

Dr. Zaidoon, "You are lying because those who were around him before his death denied it, but you did so out of hatred and greed."

Habbash: But my father told me that the land must be distributed to everyone and I am responsible for what I am saying."

Dr. Zaidoon, "Why didn't you come and tell me before you behaved in this disgraceful way. If your words are true, we are not going to hold on to the property. Give me the check and do whatever you wish with the property. I'll tell Sandus about it."

Dr. Zaidoon stood up and took the check from Habbash. He went back home and gave the check to, a good hearted, but naive Sundus. Before the conspiracy she trusted her brothers blindly. Afterwards she knew them for their truth.

She is unlike Kawthar and Zafaran. Both are very careful and do not trust easily. The most important thing is their personal interests. Although Fehmawi tried to convince his sister Zafaran to give up the property registered under her name. He visited her at home and made the offer to her.

Fehmawi, "My dear sister there are five pieces of land registered under your name. I agreed with my brothers to give you one piece and you give us the remaining four, what do you think?

Zafaran, "My dear brother, these five pieces are mine according to my father's will.

Fehmawi, "I hope you will review your decision without problems..."

Waddah interrupted, "Dear Fehmawi, she has decided to keep the five pieces of the property and any other conversation becomes meaningless. Let us not create more problems."

Fehmawi "Waddah, this issue is between us and our sister. Please do not interfere."

Zafaran, "No. My husband has the right to interfere to ensure our interest."

Waddah, "Now you have heard Zafaran's answer, and this is the final word. Please don't mention this issue in the future."

Fehmawi, "Does it means this is your final decision?

Zafaran: Yes, this is our final decision.

This conversation was exchanged in the presence of Waddah, who scolded Fehmawi. The two engaged in a verbal squabble and ended with the departure of Fehmawi.

Relations turned tense because of Sheikh Darwish's estate. The rest of the family did not receive anything from the price of the property that was relinquished by Sundus. The sale amount was divided between the sons of Sheikh Darwish. This division increased the fracture between the boys and the girls.

After a while Waddah and Dr. Zaidoon decided to spend fun time in the Iraqi hunting club founded in 1969. It includes swimming pools, food caterng and furnished celebration ballrooms. It was initially established for amateur hunters. Over time facilities for indoor-outdoor swimming pools, tennis, basketball and bowling were added. Also, there were rooms for seminars and conferences, along with large gardens where cultural, social and artistic activities were held. After touring the club's magnificent gardens, they sat down to talk.

Waddah, "Fehmawi tried to persuade Zafaran to give up the properties she had inherited, but she bravely confronted him."

Dr. Zaidoon, "If each of the boys had given up greediness and voracity, and thought about how he and his family would live a happy life, it would have been better for everyone.

Waddah, "You know, I read in a scientific journal how the world is advancing in the scopes of life."

Dr. Zaidoon, "You know the advanced world is still moving in half of the truth of existence and ignores even the search in the other half.

Waddah, "What do you mean by half reality? Where is the other half?"

Dr. Zaidoon, "We all know that life is the truth. Death is also the other truth. In other words, each share the complete truth.

Waddah, "Dr. Zaidoon, could you explain more?"

Dr. Zaidoon, "Engineer Waddah, we see the world making advances by finding everything that serves the worldly life. Meaning anything that is happening in the half-truth. The other half, which is life after death, remains neglected without much attention in the scientific research. I hope there would be scientific research in this field.

Waddah, "But, is there life after death?"

Dr. Zaidoon, "If we consider the messages brought by all the prophets, we can say "yes!". Everyone should take this potentiality into consideration.

Waddah, "But the scientific theory negates that possibility."

Dr. Zaidoon, "I believe every human being should know the messages brought by the prophets Moses, Jesus and Mohammad, and acquire an idea about that."

Waddah, "I see!"

Dr. Zaidoon, "Even true Marxism does not deny the existence of God. I have read what the famous French Marxist philosopher said in his book, (A journey to the truth), Marxism does not deny the existence of the creator. He confirmed that in his answer to a question to talk about his conversion from one extreme to another. He answered that if you mean from Marxism to Belief in the Creator! I want to explain to you that Marx himself was not an atheist. Lenin and Stalin were not accurate when they misquoted him. I studied Marxism and found that it does not negate belief in the Creator. Marxism is for organizing questions of life while belief is better because it deals with questions of life and other questions.'"

Waddah, "Do you have proofs and evidence that the universe has a Creator?"

Dr. Zaidoon, "Please notice that many scientists confirm that the universe cannot create itself. The physics scientist and universe science Mohammad Basil Altaie, sent a query to the British scientist Stephen William Hawking, who is one of the most prominent theoretical physicist and universe scientists in the world. The letter was about how the universe was created and how were its laws designed. He answered him in a letter saying, that he universe did not create itself, meaning that there is a Creator of this universe and designer of its laws. This came in an interview where the physicist scientist Mohammad Basil Altaie spoke. This is confirmed by prophets through the past times."

Waddah, "How can we realize both worldly and eternal lives at the same time."

Dr. Zaidoon, "First, by knowing God, who has no equal, then by good work in this world ie, that man lives in peace with his brother, man, and supports him in this life and give him everything that could be given, because good work is the love of people and the proper humanitarian dealing with them regardless of their beliefs and obeying the laws, and if man does not do so and dies, he comes to the eternal life and realize that it is a reality, then he will say, 'Ah, Would that I had sent forth {Good Deeds} For {this} my {Future} life'."

Waddah: What is the God's reward to the people?

Dr. Zaidoon, "Allah almighty promised man if he knew God and did good work, he would reward him in the eternal life with the Kingdom of Heaven!"

'Then shall anyone who has done an atom's weight of good, see it, and anyone who Has done an atom's weight of evil will see it.'

"The famous quote of one of the pious people."

'Work for your world as if you live forever and work for your end as if you'll die tomorrow'.

"But if man did not know God and did not do good, he would be rewarded with hell, and that is what all the prophets said."

'For those who believe and do righteous deeds, are gardens as hospitable homes for their {good} deeds.'

"It means that a pious person must do good and avoid cheating and refrain from doing bad deed in society to win the world and the eternal life."

After this conversation, they wandered into the garden of the Club and then went to work.

After a short period of lull, the Iraqi forces entered Kuwait in 1990. A few months later war broke out and the Iraqi forces were ousted from Kuwait. Economic siege of Iraq followed. The general situation got worse and the economic situation deteriorated gradually.

In this period the Iraqi government allowed a few traders to take trucks to Jordan to bring goods from Amman to Baghdad to alleviate the burden of price hike on citizens in 1991.

Some of the traders sold their truck in Jordan. When the Iraqi government knew about that. They were arrested and jailed.

Hammash contacted their relatives and took a lot of money and promised to get them out of jail.

It seems that he had gained experience in this kind of work and he had collaborators in the police department.

After two years the government took transport responsibility by sending trucks to transport goods imported from the port of Aqaba in Jordan to Baghdad to help traders. Transportation cost was not added to prices, in order to take the burden off the citizens.

An armed gang attacked some of these trucks and killed the drivers and stole the goods. This incident was repeated.

The government arrested certain gang members. Hammash contacted their relatives to defend them before the courts with a view to reduce their sentences and promised to make efforts to get them out of jail. It goes without saying that he made a lot of money as a result.

Hammash got a lot of money, by using such twisted ways at a time when the economic situation deteriorated a lot.

Meanwhile, Hamzawi traveled to London to conduct some necessary tests. His brother, Wannas, supported him.

After two weeks, the following conversation was exchanged between them. Hamzawi, "Why, brother, you spent so many years in London, to no avail."

Wannas, "I came to London in 1965 and enrolled in an English course and stayed there for six months, but I could not get the required credits to enter college. Providence wanted me to have this fate. Otherwise, I would have been buried six feet under the dust, disabled or suffering from a psychological breakdown because of the crazy wars in the country."

Hamzawi, "This was the dark period we went through. The country has lost thousands of young men the majority of which were graduates of various specializations."

Wannas, "Not speaking of the factories that discontinued production. Even the wheel of development was disrupted."

Hamzawi, "Do you intend to return to Baghdad in the future along with your family."

Wannas, "No, I have no intention to return in the present nasty environment."

Hamzawi, "We hope you will think about coming back, dear brother!"

Wannas, "My brother, I visited Baghdad in 1980 before the war, and things in Baghdad were great. The economic situation was comfortable and the development projects were in full swing to the extent that some reporters wrote that in every ten Kilometers there is a foreign company working on development projects. We looked good and the expectation was that Iraq would move at the end of the construction phase to the ranks of developed countries. As the saying goes, (The winds did not blow as the ships wish)".

The hope was that at the end of the war, that lasted eight years, the country will return to construction, but the unexpected happened. Now the economic situation is deplorable and staggering under economic sanctions. Do you expect the economic situation will improve?"

Hamzawi, "Only a miracle would improve the country's condition!"

Wannas, "My wife and I work in the clothing store that I bought. my son and daughter are at school. We are used to this kind of life and I don't think I will come back under the current circumstances."

Hamzawi, "I wish you and your family a happy life, my dear brother."

A few days later Hamzawi returned to Jordan and then by road to Baghdad. He found that nothing had changed.

The difficult economic situation has continued. All people and civil servants were affected as a whole.

Zaidoon took a vacation without pay from the university and traveled to work as a professor at a university in Jordan and in turn he sent money to his family in Iraq to be able to overcome this economic hardship. he remained there until the change took place.

CHAPTER FOUR

The invasion occurred. The Iraqi army and police forces were abolished creating a tragic catastrophe. Iraqi borders were left unprotected. The extremists rushed into Iraq from all over the world. Iraq became a hotbed for all kind of gangs.

Life in Iraq became unbearable.

At that time and under that situation, Dr. Zaidoon returned to work at the University. But life at the University was not easy.

Each week, the University hanged on the announcement board sad news. Professors were assassinated repeatedly.

Things got worse to the degree that getting to the University was an uphill task. Professors were unable to drive to the University fearing of gangs specialized in murdering professors.

Dr. Zaidoon used to go to the University in disguise, using a taxicab just as the rest of the professors did!

In this chaotic atmosphere, life in Iraq was getting worse, because of the abundant of car bombs and explosive vests.

Killing with muffled guns and armed attacks increased. Kidnapping gangs for ransom spread out. Life in the country became intolerable.

Dr. Zaidoon was attending the Cultural Society Conference. His turn came to deliver his research called (Logical Sound Thinking). He spoke saying, "Logical Sound Thinking is introducing a series of consistent, coherent and interconnected ideas that starts with a hypothesis based on a demonstrations and data, followed by a display of truths, proofs and evidence that we could support or refute. It ends with conclusions. It relies on impartial survey, followed by analysis, inference and conclusion. It features impartiality, neutrality and free of coincidences and personal whims. It distances from bias, intolerance or making pre-determined judgements."

Suddenly an explosion occurred near the Society. The conference ended and the attendees went out to examine its effects. But they were all safe from blast of a car bomb parked adjacent to the Society fence.

This was life under the shadow of these circumstances.

Hamzawi and Fehmawi worked for the tourism company until 1990, although tourism was on hold in 1985. The company began to take losses until it was liquidated. Hammash has amassed a fortune from his twisted work and still aspires to make more money by any means. Here the relationship between him and Sheikh Darwish's children began to be lukewarm, and both Hamzawi and Habbash were criticizing his actions and the methods by which he was making money.

Habbash has been in contact with his work in selling agricultural properties on the basis that they were residential plots. He continues to make money.

Before the siege of Iraq, Zafaran had sold three pieces, used Waddah's help, her husband, to build a house for them on one plot, and to build a building in the second plot, and the shops were put out for rent. As for Fehmawi, he used some farmers to cultivate some agricultural land to grow wheat, barley and rice. He took the whole crop and gave none to the other heirs. Though he still envied his sister Zafaran and her husband Waddah.

Relations between them became uncomfortable and his hatred increased when the building, that contained a number of shops, was completed. He paid three farmers to attack Waddah and punch him to teach him a lesson. As a result of being beaten he was hospitalized for three days in 2006. After being discharged from the hospital he experienced problems.

Waddah traveled to Jordan, with his wife for treatment. He passed away in an Amman hospital.

Fehmawi also traveled to Amman, to have his remaining teeth extracted, in order to build new teeth, but unfortunately this led to slow speech and an imbalance in the body. He remained in this condition until he passed away after two years.

Hamzawi remained in his home with bad health under the care of his older son.

Dr. Zaidoon has been teaching at the university and in some private colleges. He attended conferences and authored researches, despite daily harassment and difficult conditions.

In mid-April 1980 and after the end of his lectures in one of the private colleges, he stepped out to go back home in Mansour. He took a taxicab parked near the college. The driver asked for the approval of Dr. Zaidoon to stop in front of a pharmacy to pick up a prescription for his sick daughter. Dr. Zaidoon agreed. The taxi driver pretended again that his sick daughter needed the medicine. He asked again for approval to deliver the medicine to his sick daughter. Dr. Zaidoon agreed to that also. He was unaware that the driver was in fact pulling his legs. He did not realize also that a ransom kidnapping gang was waiting for him. When the cab arrived at a deserted place the driver asked for permission to deliver the medicine to his daughter in this deserted house. As he went in, a group of masked and armed men suddenly came out of the deserted house and forced Zaidoon to get out of the taxi and they brought him to the abandoned house. They tied his hands and legs to a chair. He tried to resist in no avail and asked them why he was treated with such hostility. The kidnappers told him he would know the reason soon. They blindfolded him and after a while someone appeared and said to him, "Dr. Zaidoon, welcome to our hospitality." Zaidoon replied, "Is this hospitality? Why are you treating me this way? Who are you? What do you want from me?

He replied, "Doctor, we are the mujahedeen. We have come to your country for Jihad.

Zaidoon, "Why did you come to our country and whom do you fight against?"

The kidnapper replied, "We fight the infidels."

Zaidoon, "In our country there are no infidels. All Iraqis believe in God. Why don't you go and struggle in your own country?"

Kidnapper, "The important thing is that you are here to help us fight. Call your wife to bring 10,000 dollars. We will arrange picking up the money?"

Zaidoon, "This is extortion. We can't pay that much?"

Kidnapper, "Doctor, you are able to pay the amount from your Jordanian saving account. Doctor, if you want to survive, call your wife to get the money."

Zaidoon, "What if I refuse to pay?

The Kidnapper, "In this case, you will pay a big price with your life. You would be considered an apostate and punished as such. We will rely on your books that are hostile to jihad and mujahideen."

Dr. Zaidoon, "Which book? did you read my books?"

The kidnapper replied, "No we have not read your books, but that's how it is said."

Zaidoon: "How do you consider me apostate when I believe in God and the eternal life? Most of my books are in English literature. They are academic books that have nothing to do with religion."

Kidnapper, "In our judgment, we determine who is the disbeliever, who is the believer, and what you have to do is just to shut up!"

Zaidoon, "This is determined by the Holy Book. On this basis, every human being, is a believer in nature. Therefore, it is not permissible to attack any human being, but the one who detains any human being and hinders him from doing his job is an infidel."

The kidnapper replied with annoyance by kicking Zaidoon's leg, "these are your misconceptions, keep them. Save yourself, I advise you to meet our demands."

Zaidoon, "What are your demands."

Kidnapper, "Because you refuse to give the mujahedeen what is their right. if you want to get out of here safely, I advise you to contact your wife to get the money. We will arrange collection."

Zaidoon, "Suppose my wife needs a couple of days to arrange the amount?"

Kidnapper, "In this case you will stay with us until we receive the amount."

They then contacted Sundus, Dr. Zaidoon's wife, and informed her. Sundus got confused, at the same time she received a call from Hammash who informed her of the same thing. She called her brother Hamzawi and told him the story. Hamzawi called the police. Although the police force was newly formed, they were serious about pursuing kidnapping and threatening gangs.

When Shamandar heard the news of Zaidoon's kidnapping, she drove her sister Zafaran to Sundus' house. While the car was on the road a car bomb exploded.

They were taken to the hospital and they died there.

This incident had its immense effect on the family.

On the other side, the police took the problem of Dr. Zaidoon's abduction very seriously and began to investigate until they found out the suspected hideout. The police took preparations to raid it. After two days of abduction Dr. Zaidoon was freed. Some of the kidnapers escaped. the rest were killed.

Dr. Zaidoon was liberated and returned home tired and feeling great pain in his leg. Sundus massage it until the pain subsided.

A few days after the liberation of Zaidoon from the kidnapping gang, Hammash and Kawthar decided to pay him a visit him at his home.

While they were on the road near the Tayaran Square a mine exploded burning some passing cars.

Hammash tried to avoid the explosion with no avail. His car crashed with another car. They were taken to the hospital. After a week they were discharged. Hammash lost an eye and his left foot. Kawthar came out only with only a few bruises. She lost the charm of her beauty, because of her disfigured face. This painful incident disheartened the family.

Habbash took his family and a portion of his money and managed to travel to Jordan. After a couple of days, he returned home to take the rest of his money. On his way back to Jordan a gang stopped him and carjacked his vehicle and robbed him of all the money. He was beaten up and his right arm was broken. He survived and managed to reach Jordan and stayed in the hospital to have his fractured arm treated, but the delay in treatment led to the loss of his arm. And he lived in this state with his family in Amman.

Zaidoon's health got better. He was visited by a delegate from the Minister of Higher Education to congratulate him on his safety. He carried with him the following offer to Dr. Zaidoon:

(In recognition of the high scientific position held by Dr. Zaidoon [Professor], and for publishing several research papers and a number of books in his field of specialization and for his high competence in teaching, we nominate him to the position of President of the University.)

A day later, a delegate from the Minister of Foreign Affairs visited him and carried the following offer:

(In view of his high competence in English and his knowledge of the foreign service through his book entitled [Common Terminology in Media, Politics and Diplomacy], as well as his book entitled [Diplomacy is the Beginning of Development], we nominate him as an ambassador to our country in the United States of America.)

A few days later, a delegate from the Prime Minister visited him with the following offer:

(In view of Dr. Zaidoon's competence in managing the Cultural Association of University Professors through the holding of seminars and cultural conferences, we nominate him to the position of Minister of Culture in the country.)

He had to make a choice, either approve his candidacy for the post of president of a university, ambassador in a Western country or Minister of Culture.

He has to make up his mind in two weeks.

Here we turn to the reader. If you were in Dr. Zaidoon's place what position would you chose?

AUTHOR'S BIOGRAPHY

Through the conversation with his granddaughter (who was living with cancer from 2012! But now she is ok because for excellent treated in a good hand of the hospital, doctor, nurses and even the charity people in Chicago). The Author notes through her eyes a question: Why you write your books?

Perhaps the same question in the mind of some representatives of media which contacted with the Author. So, The Author decided to talk about his Autobiography:

The Author was born in July 1945, Baghdad, Iraq. While he was in intermediate School in 1961 (Baghdad) at the evening study, registered in American Institute to learn American language, he studied in both at the same time, until he registered to be in a High School, preferring the Science Branch, after graduating from the High School, registered in The College of Arts and Sciences at the University of Almustansiriah in Baghdad/Iraq.

In the Department of English Language and Literature, then graduated from the University with BA degree (excellent). Because having an ambition to go furthermore in studying Literature Registered in the University of Wales (United Kingdom) for the postgraduate Studies,1975-1980, he got a degree of MA in English Literature, and later on got a PhD in Comparative Literature.

While He lived in United States decided to write some books to the intelligent people in the United States perhaps who likes to read and in the same time to help his middle daughter which was living couple of years with a cancer but unfortunately she was dead in London (2018) and left three kids,they are in need for the money to help them in their life specifically when their father get married .In the same time The Author 's younger (daughter living in (Jordan) with the three kids as well waiting for help specifically because her husband left to work in Iraq three years ago but unfortunately he was died in one of the explosion in Baghdad.

The Author spent over thirty years as a Professor at some Universities he was published several books there such as:

- *Dictionary of Current Idiomatic Usages, (1998)*
- *Translation with some Aspect of Application, (2002)*
- *The Development of Translation Movement in the middle Ages, (2004)*
- *Current Political and Diplomatic Idioms in Media, (2009)*
- *Originality of Translation. (2010)*
- So, he decided to write the books: the first book published in Chicago; *Charming Orient Shining England (2013)*
- And then started with the other book:
- *INTERNATIONAL NEW ARTS And SCIENCES RESEARCH JOURNAL (2014–2020),*
- *Charming Lights on the novels of Charlotte and Emily Bronte (2020)* and Learn and Develop your English in easy way (2020)

With help from his elder daughter to pay for publishing with expectations to gain enough money for helping these kids but unfortunately the Author gain nothing up to where we are right now. But he still has a hope, so he is waiting for a moment that this book *DARWISH AND HAWAZIN* is sold in order to have an enough money to help his grandsons.